The Crook and the Crown

★ Also by ★
Debbie Dadey

Mermaid Tales

Debbie Dadey

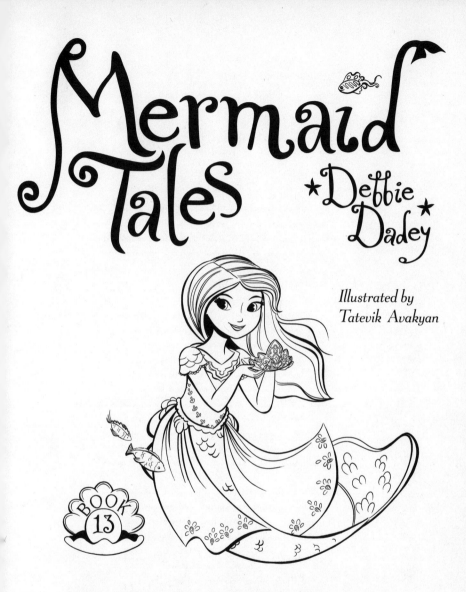

Illustrated by
Tatevik Avakyan

BOOK 13

The Crook and the Crown

ALADDIN

NEW YORK   LONDON   TORONTO   SYDNEY   NEW DELHI

ALADDIN

An imprint of Simon & Schuster Children's Publishing Division

1230 Avenue of the Americas, New York, NY 10020

This Aladdin hardcover edition December 2015

Text copyright © 2015 by Debbie Dadey

Illustrations copyright © 2015 by Tatevik Avakyan

Also available in an Aladdin paperback edition.

All rights reserved, including the right of reproduction in whole or in part in any form.

ALADDIN is a trademark of Simon & Schuster, Inc.,

and related logo is a registered trademark of Simon & Schuster, Inc.

For information about special discounts for bulk purchases,

please contact Simon & Schuster Special Sales at 1-866-506-1949

or business@simonandschuster.com.

The Simon & Schuster Speakers Bureau can bring authors to your live event.

For more information or to book an event contact the

Simon & Schuster Speakers Bureau at 1-866-248-3049

or visit our website at www.simonspeakers.com.

Series designed by Karin Paprocki

Cover designed by Karina Granda

The text of this book was set in Belucian Book.

Manufactured in the United States of America 1115 FFG

2 4 6 8 10 9 7 5 3 1

Library of Congress Control Number 2015939108

ISBN 978-1-4814-4076-9 (hc)

ISBN 978-1-4814-4075-2 (pbk)

ISBN 978-1-4814-4077-6 (eBook)

In memory of my mother,

Rebecca Ann Bailey Gibson

★ ★ ★ ★

Acknowledgments

Thank you to Laasya, Anna, as well as all my fin-tastic readers at St. Margaret's School in Woodbury Heights, New Jersey.

Contents

Fit for a Princess

H MY NEPTUNE! QUEEN Edwina sent her own royal carriage for us!" Pearl squealed.

Shelly Siren and her friends Pearl, Echo, and Kiki stood outside the Trident City People Museum as a large killer whale stopped beside them. The orca was pulling a sparkling shell carriage. Two tailmen wearing bright-blue coats with silver sashes lowered a glittering step from the carriage onto the ocean floor.

Another tailman, also wearing a blue coat, but with a gold sash, said in a loud voice, "Princess Shelly, it would be my honor to escort you

MUSEUM HOURS

and your servants to Neptune's Castle."

"Hey, we're not her servants!" Pearl snapped.

"It's all right, Pearl," Kiki said. "Let's just bubble down and enjoy the ride."

Pearl stuck her nose up in the water and frowned at

the tailman but didn't complain anymore.

Shelly hugged her grandfather good-bye before floating up the carriage's diamond-covered stairs. The inside was just as beautiful as the outside. Blue gems lined the ceiling and the seats. Shelly could see her reflection shining in the walls.

"Ooh," Pearl said, running her hand over the jeweled seats. "I've heard of this. It's aquamarine and very rare in the ocean." She turned to Shelly. "This is a carriage fit for a princess! Good thing you *are* one!"

Shelly smiled, but inside she sure didn't feel like a princess! Still, her great-aunt was Queen Edwina of the Western Oceans, and that made Shelly royalty.

As the carriage sped away, Shelly waved

to Grandfather Siren until she couldn't see him anymore. Then she sat back with a sigh. This was it! She was actually going to visit Neptune's Castle—the palace named for the very first king of the sea. When the queen had suggested that Shelly bring her friends to the castle during a school vacation, it had seemed exciting. Now it just felt scary.

Echo pushed back her dark, curly hair and turned to Shelly. "You're so quiet! Are you feeling all right?"

Shelly shrugged her blue tail. "I'm just nervous about visiting the castle. I'll be meeting all my cousins for the first time."

Even though her mother had been a princess, Shelly had only recently found out she was royal. Her parents had died when she was just a small fry, so Shelly had been raised by her grandfather in a tiny apartment in Trident City. She had never met her royal family, except for Queen Edwina.

"It's natural to be a little afraid," Kiki said. "But we'll be with you the whole time."

Shelly smiled. She knew her friends would do anything to make the visit a success.

Pearl shook her head, and her long blond hair swirled around her. "There's nothing to worry about. We're going to a castle! There will be parties and everyone will want to meet us. They're going to love me—and you, too."

Shelly nodded and tried to act happy. But inside, her stomach felt like it was full of butterflyfish. After all, she'd much rather play on a Shell Wars team than wear a frilly party dress. And she wasn't sure if she could do the things a princess was supposed to do. What if she wasn't royal enough for her relatives?

Shelly's thoughts were interrupted by a squeal.

"Sweet seaweed!" Pearl gasped. "We're being invaded!"

2

Screech, Click, Squeal!

THE MERGIRLS LOOKED OUT the carriage window. They were surrounded by huge black-and-white killer whales!

"There are at least fifteen of them," Echo said, her dark eyes wide.

"They're going to kill us!" Pearl screeched.

Kiki shook her head. "Killer whales have never attacked merfolk before."

"Maybe they plan to start with us," Pearl said nervously, pushing away from the window and closing her eyes.

"I think they're beautiful," Shelly said, leaning out the carriage window to watch the enormous creatures. Their fins were taller than her grandfather!

"Did you know that killer whales actually aren't whales at all?" Kiki told them. "They're the biggest of the dolphins."

"Did you know that I don't care?" Pearl snapped, her eyes still closed. "They're scary no matter what they are called!"

Suddenly, loud squealing noises filled the air.

Pearl put her hands over her ears. "What is that horrible racket?"

"The orcas are talking to one another," Shelly explained before making the same whistling noise. "They came to say hello!"

Kiki, Echo, and Pearl stared at Shelly in surprise.

"You know how to speak killer whale?" Kiki asked.

When Shelly nodded, Kiki said, "No wavy way! You have to teach me."

"Sure," Shelly said. She made a screech, followed by a click. "This means hello, nice to meet you." Kiki tried to do the same.

Even Echo gave it a try, but Pearl frowned and sat with her ears covered, humming the newest song by the popular merboy band, the Rays.

A chorus of sounds answered Shelly. She waved at the crowd of orcas near the carriage.

The killer whale pulling their carriage let out an especially loud whistle, and Shelly gulped. "We're almost there," she told her merfriends. "Our orca said to look to the right."

The mergirls leaned over to gaze out the window, and Shelly let out a cry.

"Oh my Neptune!"

"What's wrong?" Echo asked, peering over Shelly's shoulder. "It's beautiful!"

"It's enormous," Kiki said with a gulp.

Shelly nodded. "I knew it would be big, but this is grander than I ever dreamed."

All four mergirls stared out the windows as their carriage glided past large stone posts with fire spouting from them. Rows of spectacular seaweed formed paths that were dotted with statues, bubbling fountains, and coral displays. The gardens alone were overwhelming, but they led to a glistening castle that took Shelly's breath away.

Pearl gasped. "This is a mermillion times better than the drawings I've seen in *MerStyle* magazine. Check out that tower!"

Shelly looked up and down and all

around. The palace had so many round buildings and domed roofs it was hard to take them all in. This was Neptune's famous castle! She couldn't believe she was in the place where the first king of the sea had lived many mercenturies ago.

"The windows really *are* made of blue sapphires—just like Mrs. Karp told us when we studied jewels," Kiki said.

A long line of merpeople stood in front of the large bronze castle door.

"Do you think those are my relatives?" Shelly whispered as their carriage slowed, then came to a stop.

Pearl shook her head. "No, those are probably the queen's merservants welcoming you." It was then that Shelly noticed

the merpeople were wearing royal uni-
forms, some with aprons.

"But there are hundreds of them!" Echo
told Pearl.

"Well, it is a big castle," Kiki said with
a giggle.

Shelly looked at Kiki, and they both
laughed. Echo chuckled too, but Pearl
snapped her fingers. "This is no time
for silliness. Inside the palace will be
another line of people for you to meet—
your royal family! Don't forget to curtsy
to them."

Shelly stopped laughing. This was it!
She was about to meet her many cousins.
Her mind swirled with thoughts. What
if they didn't like her? What if she wasn't

royal enough? Did they know she had grown up in a tiny apartment instead of a gigantic castle? Suddenly Shelly wished more than anything that she had stayed home with her grandfather.

A Crown of Jewels

I 'M SCARED," SHE WHISPERED.

Echo looked nervous too, but she still squeezed Shelly's hand. "Don't worry, we're all here for you."

Shelly took a deep breath and floated outside the carriage.

A chorus of voices greeted her. "All hail Princess Shelly!"

Shelly was so surprised she fell backward. Pearl helped her up and whispered, "Start waving!"

Shelly remembered how her aunt had waved and nodded to the crowd when she'd visited Trident City. Shelly did the same.

As she and her merfriends floated toward the door, the many merservants bowed or curtsied. When they arrived at the castle's huge bronze doors, Shelly held her breath.

All at once, the doors flew open and Queen Edwina gathered Shelly in her arms. "Welcome, Princess Shelly! We are delighted to have you and your friends visit Neptune's Castle. Let me introduce you to your many cousins."

A large crowd of mergirls, merboys, merwomen, and mermen bowed and curtsied as Queen Edwina called each of their names: Princess Cora, Princess Corinne, Princess Corrisa, Princess Sapphire, Princess Sephira, Prince Gifford, Prince Fritz, Princess Brenna, Prince Fami, Princess Rosa, Prince Yaron, Princess Daphne, Prince Nils, Prince Dimitri, and Prince Orly. Shelly's head spun, trying to remember all the names.

Finally, the Queen reached the very last one. As Shelly stared at her youngest cousin, she knew she would never forget her name: Princess Lorelei.

Lorelei smiled at Shelly and did a little curtsy. Shelly did the same, but she couldn't take her eyes off Lorelei's face.

"No wavy way!" Echo whispered in Shelly's ear. "You two look exactly alike!"

Queen Edwina held up her hand, and immediately a servant appeared with a fluffy piece of pillow lava. Perched on top was a sparkling silver tiara. Several cousins, including Lorelei, exclaimed aloud when they saw the small crown.

The crowd murmured as Queen Edwina placed it on Shelly's head. "This is the Crown of Joy. It was my very first tiara. It was also your mother's first tiara, and now I want it to be yours."

Shelly thought she saw a tear in Queen Edwina's eye. She couldn't believe her mother had once worn this very crown. Shelly felt like crying herself, but she was pretty sure princesses weren't supposed to to bawl in public. So she bit her lip and smiled. "Thank you so much. It is beautiful!"

"Of course! Every princess must have a tiara to wear to royal dinners and events," Queen Edwina said with a smile. "Now, you're probably quite tired from your morning's journey! Thatcher will show you to your room."

As the queen's personal tailman led the mergirls up a wide marble staircase, Shelly's tail caught on a step and she fell forward. The tiara tumbled off her head, but luckily, Pearl caught it before it fell to the ground.

"That crown is worth more than all the jewels in Trident City!" Pearl squealed. "Be careful with it!"

Shelly put the tiara firmly back on her

head. When she'd first come to the castle, she'd been frightened her cousins wouldn't like her. Now she had something else to worry about: making sure she didn't break the Crown of Joy!

4

Zee Royal Tailor

THIS DAY JUST KEEPS GETTING better and better!" Pearl shrieked. "We get to live in the best room ever for our entire trip!"

Shelly felt like she was in a dream. She sat on her huge breadcrumb sponge bed and looked around their circular room. The ceiling was filled with pictures made from brightly colored pieces of polished glass. Furniture carved from shells and studded with rubies and emeralds made the room look quite fancy. There was even a big glass mirror in the corner. Four bedrooms surrounded the main room, each a different color to match their tails—blue for Shelly, pink for Echo, purple for Kiki, and gold for Pearl. Glittering seaweed curtains decorated with beach morning glories and pink pearls hung in each doorway. The curtains were pulled back so the bedrooms were open to the main living room. It was perfect!

"I can't believe how soft this sponge

pillow is," Echo said, floating over to Shelly. Then Echo grinned and swung her pillow at Kiki.

Kiki laughed. "Pillow fight!" With seventeen brothers, Kiki had probably had plenty of pillow fight practice. She bopped Pearl in the nose with her pillow.

Shelly very carefully put the Crown of Joy on the shell table beside her bed. Then she joined in the fun by smacking Echo's tail with her pillow.

Before long all the mergirls were on Shelly's bed, whacking one another with pillows and giggling. Bits of sponge fell and floated around the room.

"What is going on here?!" screeched an angry voice. An elderly servant stood in the middle of the room, frowning at the kelp comforter that had been tossed off Shelly's bed.

"Sorry!" Shelly said. "We'll straighten this up."

As the girls scrambled to fix the bed, the servant introduced herself. "I am Helga, the head housekeeper. I run this castle with an iron tail." She slapped her green tail on the marble floor.

"Hey, you can't talk to us—" Pearl started to say, but Helga interrupted her.

"You royals are all alike," she grumbled. "You just come here to cause trouble for the queen."

Shelly shook her head and opened her mouth, but Helga didn't give Shelly a chance to speak. "You mess up the joust-ing ring, wear out the sea horses, litter the picnic grounds, and dance the night away." Helga jammed her thumb into her chest. "But Helga knows everything that goes on inside this castle, so don't try to pull anything over on Helga!" She shook her head and swam away, muttering angrily as she went.

Just before she reached the door, Helga turned and looked at Shelly. "With all this mischief, I almost forgot! You and your merfriends are to be fitted for gowns. The royal tailor will be in shortly to take your measurements."

Helga slammed the door behind her so hard that the shell furniture rattled. The four mergirls looked at one another before bursting into giggles.

"I guess everything *isn't* perfect here at the castle," Shelly said.

Pearl put her hands on her hips. "That Helga is grumpier than Mr. Fangtooth!" Mr. Fangtooth was a cafeteria worker at their school who was known for being very cranky. "Don't let her talk to you that way," Pearl told Shelly. "After all, you are a princess."

Shelly shrugged. She still didn't feel like a princess. Instead of being fitted for a gown, she'd much rather be out in the ocean, exploring caves. But she didn't say anything, because a tall, skinny merman wearing a long purple robe burst into the room, followed by several assistants.

"Hellooò, merladies! My name eez François. You are about to be dazzled by *moi*, zee royal tailor!" François exclaimed, flinging his hands around.

"Hi," Shelly said. "My name is Shelly."

"*Princess* Shelly," Pearl added. "And I'm Pearl. This is Echo and Kiki."

"Oh darling!" François said with a frown at Shelly. "We simply must do something about zees hair."

"But I like my red hair," Shelly said softly.

"What's not to like, my pet? 'Tis like zee queen's," he said. "But we must match it to your gown—and I didn't bring zee right fabric." He clapped his hands, and his assistants scurried away. They were back in seconds with different pieces of sparkling kelp.

François held up a piece. "Mmm, zees is lovely. Actually, zees would make a mervelous mersuit for *moi*, don't you agree?!" he asked Kiki, holding it up to his waist. "I do love beautiful things."

Kiki nodded, but Pearl snapped, "Hey! What about our gowns?"

"Of course," François said, glaring at Pearl. He looked at each mergirl and then studied the fabric in front of him. He tapped his chin twice with his tail and clapped his hands.

"I have made zee decision!" He held up four glittery scraps of kelp. "Zees goes with red hair, zees with curly hair, zees with black hair, and zees with zee blond hair."

His assistants swooped up the pieces and swiftly wrapped each girl in the correct one. They draped and measured until the tailor clapped his hands once more.

"Enough! We must be away," François said. "I have an important appointment I cannot miss!"

"But when will our gowns be ready?" Pearl demanded.

"Do not fret! They will be zee most beautiful dresses you have ever seen," François said as he and his assistants soared out of the room. "You will have them in time for zee royal ball tomorrow night."

"Ball?" Shelly squeaked. "You can't wear gowns to throw a ball around!"

"I think he's talking about a dance," Kiki said.

Pearl nodded. "A fancy dance."

"But I don't even know how to dance," Shelly said, feeling butterflyfish in her stomach again.

"Don't worry," Echo said. "I'll teach you."

Shelly nodded. "Okay," she agreed. She decided not to think about the ball just yet. "So what do you want to do now?"

"Ride sea horses," Echo blurted.

"Visit the ballroom!" Pearl shouted.

"See the royal library?" Kiki suggested.

Unfortunately, they all spoke at the same time. Shelly looked around at her friends' disappointed faces. No one liked anyone else's suggestions.

Shelly rubbed her forehead. One thing was for sure, this was going to be one long visit if they couldn't agree. What was she going to do?

Saddle Up, Sea Horse!

HELLY PUT ONE HAND BEHIND her back. "Whoever guesses how many fingers I'm holding up gets to pick what we'll do."

"Five," Pearl said immediately.

"Two?" Echo said.

Kiki held up one finger.

Shelly pulled her hand out to show that she had two fingers up.

"Yes!" Echo cheered.

Pearl protested, but followed her friends to the door. Before she left, Shelly made sure the Crown of Joy was sitting where she had left it. She didn't want to risk it falling off while she rode a sea horse. She smiled when she saw it gleaming on her bedside table.

When they arrived at King Neptune's stables, they found rows of beautifully groomed sea horses chomping away on tiny shrimp. Shelly was surprised to see her cousin Lorelei at the stables. She wore a bright-blue riding outfit and a matching helmet, and she was brushing the mane of an orange sea horse.

Lorelei smiled and waved. "Hi, Shelly!" she said. "Nice to see you again."

"Hi!" Shelly said. It felt so strange to look at Lorelei—like looking into the mirror in their royal room! "These are my friends Echo, Pearl, and Kiki. We'd like to take the sea horses for a ride!"

"Wave-tastic!" Lorelei said with a smile. "Why don't you ride my favorite, Champion?" She patted the orange sea horse. The horse snorted and nuzzled Lorelei's hand.

"Thanks," Shelly said, petting Champion.

"You're not wearing the Crown of Joy," Lorelei said, staring at Shelly's hair.

Shelly shook her head. "I didn't want to lose it. It's a very special tiara."

"Yes, it is," Lorelei agreed, biting her lip. "It's the queen's favorite one, you know." Lorelei looked upset, and Shelly didn't know what to say.

Thankfully, Lorelei seemed to cheer up right away and smiled at Shelly. "I'm so happy to finally meet you," Lorelei said. "There aren't many cousins our age in the castle. It gets lonely around here."

Shelly grinned just as Echo giggled. A bright-pink sea horse gulped a tiny shrimp right from Echo's hand. "She's so cute and sweet," Echo said, patting the sea horse's head.

"Why don't you ride with us?" Shelly asked Lorelei.

Lorelei shook her head. "I just finished

a little ride, and I have to get back to the castle or my mom will have my tail! But if you take that trail"—she pointed toward a path made of broken seashells—"you can't get lost. And at the end is an awesome whirlpool."

"I've read about whirlpools," Kiki said nervously. "They're supposed to be very pretty, but they can be dangerous."

Lorelei patted Kiki's arm. "As long as you stay on the trail, you'll be perfectly safe. It is totally wave-tastic! Just don't get too close or . . ."

"We'll be sucked in?" Kiki said with a gulp.

"That won't happen!" Lorelei assured her.

"Yee-haw!" Echo said as she swung into the saddle of the bright-pink sea horse.

"Yee-haw?" Shelly said. "What does that mean?"

Echo shrugged. "I'm not sure, but Rocky told me that humans say it when they ride horses. He also told me 'giddyup' means go and 'whoa' means stop." Echo loved everything about humans.

Pearl sniffed the water around a purple

sea horse and held her nose. "Pee-ew! Are you sure these things are safe? They stink!"

"Of course! I ride every day," Lorelei told Pearl. "That horse is the rarest breed. It's very valuable."

"Well, in that case," Pearl said, "yee-haw!"

All four mergirls waved good-bye to Lorelei and followed the trail, which circled a pretty outcropping of cold-water coral. As they rode, Shelly pointed out a big school of bluecheek butterflyfish fluttering just above them.

"Hey, I think I'm getting the hang of this," Pearl said. But she almost fell off her sea horse when a shiny fish zipped past her.

"What was that?" she screeched.

Kiki peered into the water. "I think that was a dolphinfish."

"Well, it needs to learn some manners," Pearl snapped.

When the calm waters started to swirl around them, Shelly shouted, "We must be getting close to the whirlpool!"

"Maybe we should head back," Kiki said quietly.

"Just stay on the trail," Shelly told her friends. "I don't think we'll want to miss this!"

As the four mergirls rounded a bend, they couldn't believe their eyes. In the distance, the water swirled around and around. It churned and bubbled like someone was twirling it with a big hand.

"Wow! If you were sucked up in that, you'd never make it out," Echo said softly.

"It's so pretty," Shelly said.

"Pretty scary, if you ask me!" Pearl squealed. "So we've seen it! Now, I vote we leave."

No one argued, and the four mergirls turned their sea horses back toward the stables.

After they had unharnessed, fed, and brushed their horses, the four merfriends swam back to the castle.

Kiki fell onto a huge sponge sofa with a dreamy sigh. "This place is the best." She turned to Shelly. "I still can't believe Queen Edwina gave you her favorite tiara," she said. "That's totally wavy."

"I know!" Pearl squealed. "Why don't you let us try it on? We can pretend we're princesses too!"

"Sure," Shelly said. "As long as you're careful." She swam over to the small table where she'd left the Crown of Joy—and screamed.

"What's wrong?" Echo asked, rushing to Shelly's side.

Shelly pointed to the empty spot. "It's gone!"

6

Tiara Trouble

ID YOU MOVE IT?" ECHO asked, tapping her pink tail on the marble floor.

Shelly shook her head. "When we left for the stables, it was right there," she said, pointing to her bedside table.

The mergirls searched every closet,

under every bed, and in every dresser drawer. They turned the entire royal suite upside down, but the Crown of Joy was nowhere to be found.

"Could someone have taken it?" Pearl asked.

"Who would do such a thing?" Kiki asked.

"Well, horrible Helga was mean to us," Pearl said with a frown. "Maybe she did!"

Shelly knew Helga was grouchy, but she seemed very dedicated to Queen Edwina. "I don't think she would do that," Shelly said.

"Well, then who?" Pearl asked impatiently.

"What about the tailor?" Echo suggested.

Pearl clapped her hands. "That's right.

François *did* say he liked beautiful things. And that tiara is fabulously pretty!"

Shelly tried to imagine François wearing the Crown of Joy, but she couldn't. "We would have noticed if he'd taken it."

"But we were gone for quite a while. Maybe he snuck back in and took it then," Kiki said slowly. "You're sure it was here before you left, Shelly?"

Shelly nodded. "Yes, I'm sure."

Echo piped up. "That means the thief must have struck this afternoon!"

Kiki snapped her fingers. "I've read a lot of mystery books," she told them, "so I know all about investigating crimes. First we need to question our suspects. Let's start with François!"

Shelly hated to think that either François or Helga might have stolen the Crown of Joy, and she knew it wasn't nice to accuse other merfolk. But then she thought about how upset Queen Edwina would be when she discovered it was missing.

"Okay," Shelly agreed. "Let's find him."

The mergirls zoomed out into the hallway before screeching to a stop. "Excuse me, but where can we find François, the tailor?" Kiki asked a merservant passing by.

The merservant, who carried a huge stack of kelp sheets, bowed to the girls. "My merladies, you can find the tailor downstairs, just past the ballroom."

"Thanks!" Shelly said. The mergirls sped away but slowed down when they got close to the tailor's room.

"We have to be sneaky," Pearl warned them.

They tipfinned their way to François's door and peered inside. The tailor and his assistants were working furiously on the gowns. Kelp fabric was everywhere. Shiny ribbons and shells covered a table. Shelly's eyes searched the small room, but there wasn't a tiara anywhere.

Kiki took a deep breath and tapped on the door. "Excuse me, Mr. François," she said, whipping out a piece of kelp and a sea pen. "May I ask you a few questions?"

François jumped up at the sight of the

mergirls. "Oh, hello!" He looked down at the table, then glanced around nervously. "As you can see, we are very, very bizee here. Lots to do before zee big ball!"

Shelly spoke up shyly. "Yes, but this is important." She didn't know what else to say. She didn't want François to know that the Crown of Joy was missing.

"Where were you this afternoon?" Pearl blurted.

François's cheeks turned bright red. "Zat eez none of your beezniss!" he shrieked. He darted out of the room before anyone could stop him.

"Oh no!" Shelly said. "I hope we didn't upset him."

One of François's assistants, a merwoman

with bright-purple hair, approached the mergirls. "Don't worry," she said. "François is just a little embarrassed." She looked around and lowered her voice. "Every afternoon he takes splash dance lessons in the royal ballroom. He doesn't want anyone to know about it! He was a terrible dancer before he started the lessons."

"Okay," Shelly told the assistant. "Thanks for letting us know!"

When the mergirls got back to their room, Shelly was more upset than ever. "François definitely didn't take the tiara if he was splash dancing," she moaned. "That means it's really gone."

"No, that means Helga took it," Pearl declared. "She's the only suspect left!"

"She's right," Echo said with a shrug. "It does look like Helga stole it."

Kiki shook her head. "We don't have any proof that Helga did it."

Shelly knew Kiki was right. They couldn't accuse Helga of taking the Crown of Joy just because she'd been mean to them.

But if Helga hadn't taken it, who had?

Seat of Honor

THAT EVENING SHELLY, PEARL, Echo, and Kiki were summoned to the royal dining room for dinner. Shelly was sick with worry. She didn't want to tell her aunt the Crown of Joy was missing.

"Oh my Neptune!" Echo said with a

gulp as they entered the mervelous dining room. "This table is longer than Trident City's main street!"

It was definitely the biggest table Shelly had ever seen. Each side was lined with cousins, all wearing small crowns. But none of their crowns were as beautiful as Shelly's lost tiara. Thatcher appeared at Shelly's elbow. "Her Royal Majesty requests that you dine with her this evening."

Shelly nodded. "We were just going to sit down." Echo, Pearl, and Kiki each pulled out a heavy shell chair that was inlaid with diamonds in a penguin pattern.

Thatcher shook his head and pointed toward Shelly's aunt at the other end of the table. "Queen Edwina would like you to join her there."

"Oh no," Shelly said softly.

"Pardon me?" Thatcher said.

Pearl put her arm around Shelly's shoulders and turned to Thatcher. "We would be delighted to feast with the queen."

"Maybe she won't notice that you're not wearing the tiara," Echo whispered.

Shelly crossed her tail fins and hoped that Echo was right. As they swam over to take their seats, Shelly noticed Lorelei sitting in the chair next to the queen.

"Lorelei, angelfish, why don't you switch seats with Princess Shelly?" Queen Edwina suggested. "I would love to spend some time with her."

Lorelei looked hurt but nodded. "Of course, Auntie," she said softly.

Shelly felt horrible that Lorelei had to change seats, but before she could protest, Queen Edwina said, "Shelly! Where is the Crown of Joy?"

Shelly's mouth opened, but nothing came out. How could she tell Queen Edwina that she'd lost the tiara?

"She . . . is saving it to wear to the ball tomorrow," Kiki told the queen.

Queen Edwina smiled. "Oh, very clever idea! You will make a grand entrance with that lovely crown!"

After the mergirls sat down, plates piled with strange-looking food appeared in front of them. "What is this?" Shelly whispered to Lorelei.

"That's rabbitfish steak with beluga sturgeon sauce," Lorelei replied. "It's delicious!"

Shelly bit into the steak. The sauce was filled with round black balls that tasted very salty. She wanted to spit them out, but she forced herself to swallow them.

"Try some of this tarpon tea," Kiki suggested. "It's even better than my family's comb jelly tea."

Shelly sipped the tea from a shell cup. It was fin-tastic!

While the mergirls feasted on balsamic bonefish with petite ladyfish croutons and candied gulper eel wrapped in Irish moss, Queen Edwina spoke more about the Crown of Joy. She told them all about how Shelly's mother had worn it to her very first ball, the same dance where she had met Shelly's father.

"They were married shortly after that," the Queen finished.

Shelly wiped a tear from her eye. She loved hearing stories about her parents. She tried to imagine them as young merfolk, meeting for the very first time. Had her mother liked balls? Or had she felt uncomfortable in dresses, like Shelly did?

Shelly was thinking so much about her parents that she accidentally bumped her

cup against the table. The delicate shell shattered into pieces.

"Oh no!" Shelly gasped. A dark shadow fell over her. She looked up into Helga's angry eyes. "I'm so sorry, Helga. I will clean this up right away."

"Nonsense!" Queen Edwina said, waving her arm. "You are my special guest! Helga will take care of it."

Throughout the rest of the meal, Helga glared at Shelly. When Queen Edwina excused herself to attend to royal business, Helga hissed into Shelly's ear, "I'll say it again: You royals are nothing but trouble!"

Pearl looked at Shelly and raised an eyebrow. "Trouble my tail!" Pearl said. "Don't listen to a word Helga says!"

But by the time their flaming coral-weed cake arrived for dessert, Shelly had lost her appetite. If Helga hadn't hated her before, Shelly was sure she did now.

8

A Royal Review

I T'S SETTLED! HELGA DEFINITELY took the crown!" Pearl declared when they got back to their room after dinner. Shelly shook her head and sat down on her soft blue bed. Suddenly she was very tired and just wanted to be home. "We don't know that for sure."

"Helga does look awfully guilty," Echo said. "Why else would she be so mean to you?"

"I read in *MerStyle* that long ago servants tried to steal the royal trident!" Pearl announced. "Maybe Helga is trying to do the very same thing with the crown."

"Did they get away with it?" Kiki asked. The royal trident was King Neptune's pointed stick, which Queen Edwina now carried. It was said to have magical powers.

"Nope. A royal guard caught them before they could snatch it," Pearl replied.

"Maybe we should speak to the royal guards," Echo suggested with a yawn.

Kiki nodded. "I still don't think Helga

took it, but it can't hurt to ask the guards if they've seen anything. It's too late now, so let's visit them first thing tomorrow."

The mergirls settled into their beds: Shelly in the blue one, Pearl in the gold, Echo in the pink, and Kiki in the pur-ple. They left the curtains open so they could see one another. Queen Edwina had gone to a lot of trouble making sure their bedrooms were just right. All Shelly could think about was how upset the queen would be when she discovered the tiara was lost.

Shelly felt like she was running out of time! The ball was tomorrow night, and the queen would surely notice that Shelly wasn't wearing the Crown of Joy.

She tossed and turned in her soft sponge bed. It was very late before she finally fell asleep.

THE NEXT MORNING SHELLY AWOKE TO find that François had delivered their beautiful ball gowns. Kiki, Echo, and Pearl were excited, but Shelly faked a smile. How could she be happy about the ball with the Crown of Joy still missing? She was so worried she couldn't think straight.

Pearl immediately pulled her gold gown over her head. Beautiful sparkling shells decorated the top and bottom of the dress. "These are the most sea-tacular party dresses ever!" she squealed. "I can't wait to wear mine tonight!"

Echo put her hand on Shelly's shoulder. "Maybe we should skip the ball," Echo suggested.

Kiki nodded. "I don't think Shelly feels up to it."

"Skip the ball?" Pearl snapped. She whirled around from the mirror, where she had been admiring her reflection. "Just because Shelly is upset doesn't mean we should *all* suffer. Besides, the queen is giving the ball in our honor. It would be rude not to show up."

Shelly took a deep breath and nodded. "Pearl's right. We have to go. I must tell Queen Edwina the truth."

"We may still find the tiara," Kiki said. "There's plenty of time before the ball tonight. In fact, let's ask the royal guards right now. They'll know what to do!"

Pearl slowly pulled off her gown and laid it on her bed. "Fine," she said grumpily.

ANOTHER HELPFUL SERVANT POINTED the mergirls in the direction of the royal guards' office. On the way, they passed a clownfish juggling sea potatoes. Even though she was upset, Shelly couldn't help laughing.

"That's amazing," Echo said, pointing

to the clownfish. "This castle really does have everything."

Before they could swim any farther, three tailmen appeared before them, followed by Queen Edwina.

"There you are, Princess Shelly!" she exclaimed. "I've had Thatcher looking everywhere for you. I want to take you and your merfriends for a royal review of the palace grounds, the water polo fields, and the many gardens."

"But Your Highness, we were on our way to the—" Echo started to tell the queen.

Pearl interrupted Echo. "We would be delighted to go on a royal review with you, Your Majesty."

"Of course," Shelly said. "It is very

kind of you to take time out of your busy schedule to show us around." She guessed they'd have to visit the royal guards after the tour.

Just then Lorelei floated over to them. She was wearing a white tailsuit and carrying a long, pointed sword.

She waved to Shelly, Kiki, Echo, and Pearl, then curtsied to the queen. "Auntie, I've been waiting for you at the jousting ring. Did you forget our fencing lesson today?"

Fencing? Shelly was shocked. She couldn't believe the queen played with swords!

Shelly's aunt must have noticed Shelly's surprised look, because she chuckled. "Yes, it's true! I'm not only queen, I'm also a fencing champion. And I've been giving Lorelei lessons." She patted Lorelei on her shoulder. "But since this is Princess Shelly's first trip to Neptune's Castle, I'd like to spend the afternoon showing her the palace grounds. We can resume our lessons next week."

Lorelei looked disappointed. "Okay," she said softly, and floated away, leaving a trail of sad bubbles behind her.

Shelly felt terrible. "Please, Aunt Edwina," she said. "I don't want Lorelei to miss her lesson! We can do the royal review another time."

"I won't hear of it! It's not every day my great-niece comes for a visit," Queen Edwina told Shelly. "Now, let's begin. We have much to see!"

As they floated down a path outside

the castle, Queen Edwina said, "There's the statue of Alanna. That's where King Rudolph asked me to marry him."

"So romantic," Pearl said. Echo sighed dreamily. Alanna was a mermaid who had fallen in love with a human. She'd also been the first to encourage laws saying merfolk should not hurt humans.

"I'm sorry King Rudolph isn't here, but he couldn't miss the Vortex Water Polo charity event this year," Queen Edwina explained. "He sends his greetings and looks forward to meeting you another time."

Shelly nodded. "Please tell him I said hello."

"Wow!" Echo cried. "Look at that!" She pointed to a large waterfall.

"Isn't it unique?" Queen Edwina said. "And such a pretty sight."

She turned to Shelly. "Now I'd like to show you our Shell Wars and water polo fields. I hear you are quite the athlete."

Shelly nodded. "I do play Shell Wars on the Trident Academy team."

"Hopefully you will play here someday," the queen said.

As fun as it was, Shelly hoped that the tour would end soon. The mergirls still hadn't visited the royal guards! Shelly tried to act interested in the rolling kelp fields, but all she could think about was the missing Crown of Joy.

She thought about it during lunch at the Coral Reef Café. She thought about it while they watched a water polo match. She thought about it during their visit to each of the palace's beautiful gardens. Shelly's favorite was a hidden garden almost completely surrounded by enormous clumps of hump coral.

By the end of the afternoon, Shelly felt desperate. When the queen finally dismissed the girls, they raced to the royal guards' office, but it was too late! A sign posted on the door read CLOSED.

"Oh no," Shelly said softly.

"It'll be all right," Echo said as they swam back to their room. It was time to get ready for the ball!

9

Picture Perfect

PEARL ADMIRED HER WORK. "Wow. I'm splashing good, if I do say so myself," she said.

"Let me see," Echo said, swimming around to see what Pearl had done to Shelly's long red hair. "Ooh, it looks fin-tastic!"

Kiki nodded. "Mervelous!"

The mergirls were in their room, getting ready for the ball. Each wore a beautiful gown that matched the color of their tails.

Shelly smiled at her reflection in the mirror. Pearl had twisted Shelly's hair around the top of her head and then tucked sea lavender all around. "Isn't this Queen Edwina's favorite flower?" Shelly asked.

Pearl nodded. "Of course! Maybe she'll be so tickled by it that she won't notice the Crown of Joy is missing."

Shelly stopped smiling. She knew she'd have to tell Queen Edwina the truth, even if the queen didn't notice. But Shelly didn't want to ruin everyone's fun. "You all look so pretty. I wish I had one of those human objects that could take your picture."

Fortunately, Queen Edwina had thought of everything. As soon as the girls had finished getting ready, a tap sounded at their door. It was the royal artist!

"Greetings, merladies," he said. "My name is Collins. The queen sent me to draw your portrait."

Pearl clapped her hands.

"Now," said Collins, "I need Princess Shelly to sit in the center while her mermaids-in-waiting float around her."

"We are her merfriends!" Pearl snapped. "Not her mermaids-in-waiting."

The artist nodded. "Of course. You are

all very lovely. Please strike a pose and hold still."

As Collins sketched their portrait on a large piece of kelp, Shelly tried to ignore the itch on the tip of her nose. Finally she couldn't wait. She had to scratch! She did it quickly, but it didn't matter because the artist said, "Ta-da! I'm finished!"

"That was fast!" Echo exclaimed. The four mergirls floated around to see the picture. Collins had drawn them perfectly.

"Ooh, Collins, you are shelltacular!" Pearl said.

Collins took a bow and told them, "I will make copies for each of you to take home, courtesy of Her Majesty."

"My parents are going to love that," Echo said.

Shelly nodded, but she couldn't stop staring at the portrait, especially her hair. The flowers were pretty, but they weren't a tiara.

"Enough fussing in here!" Helga's voice boomed as she barged into the room. "It's time to go! The ball is about to begin!" She thumped her tail on the floor impatiently.

Shelly gasped. "But I'm not ready!"

Echo gave her a hug. "Don't worry about anything. Your aunt loves you. She'll understand."

Pearl glared at Helga. "And we'll finally tell the queen what *really* happened!"

10

Belles of the Ball

ANNOUNCING THE ARRIVAL of Her Royal Highness, Princess Shelly of the Western Oceans, from the ancient lineage of Cronus, and daughter of the Duchess of the Galapagos Rise, Princess Lenore," Thatcher proclaimed as Shelly stood at

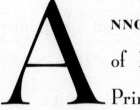

the top of a marble staircase. A conch shell sounded, and hundreds of mer-people in the ballroom clapped. Shelly saw Lorelei staring at her with a look of surprise. Many cousins frowned. All of them stared at the top of Shelly's head, where the Crown of Joy should have been!

Pearl nudged Shelly, reminding her to nod and wave.

Thatcher read aloud from a kelp note in his hand. "Announcing the arrival of Merlady Echo, Merlady Kiki, and Merlady Pearl. They are ambassadors from Trident Academy." Echo, Kiki, and Pearl smiled and waved.

"Wow, that was quite an introduction,"

Echo whispered after they'd all floated to the bottom of the steps.

Pearl giggled. "Did you hear him call us merladies? I can't wait to tell my mother. She's going to faint!"

When Queen Edwina glided over, Shelly felt like she might pass out herself. "You all look so lovely," the queen said with a smile. She leaned in to examine Shelly's hair. "Shelly, I love those flowers, but where is the Crown of Joy? I thought you were saving it for tonight."

Tears filled Shelly's eyes. How could she tell her aunt the tiara was gone?

Pearl put her arm around Shelly and faced the queen. "Your Highness, something very strange has happened," Pearl began.

"And what is that?" the queen asked.

"Well," Pearl said slowly, "somehow the Crown of Joy was misplaced. It—it is missing."

The queen fainted, but luckily, two royal guards caught her. "Aunt Edwina, are you okay?" Shelly cried.

The queen opened her eyes as another merservant brought a chair for her to sit in. "How could you? That tiara belonged to my great-grandmother!" the queen said with a gasp. "It is irreplaceable!"

Tears streamed down Shelly's cheeks. "I'm so sorry!" she whispered.

Shelly didn't know what to do, so she turned and fled. She could hear her friends calling after her, but she ignored them.

Shelly didn't stop swimming for a long time. Finally she found herself treading water at the sea horse stables, where she collapsed and cried. The soft neighs and whinnies of the horses soothed her.

Many merminutes passed before Shelly heard a voice. It was Echo!

"There you are! We've been looking all over for you." Echo floated into the stables, followed by Kiki and Pearl.

Pearl held her nose. "Ew!" she muttered. "Sea horse stink cannot be good for my beautiful gown!"

Shelly wiped her eyes. "I know I shouldn't

have left like that, but I didn't know what else to do. I can't face the queen!"

"It was very rude of you," Pearl told her, only it sounded funny because Pearl was still holding her nose.

"Please come back," Kiki said. "The queen is worried about you."

"We have to tell her that Helga took the Crown of Joy!" Echo added.

Shelly shook her head. "That's not right. We can't be sure Helga took it!"

Pearl rolled her eyes. "She's been mean to you ever since we've been here."

"But that doesn't mean she stole the crown," Shelly insisted.

Kiki nodded. "Shelly's right. We don't have any proof."

"Never mind," Pearl said impatiently. "We have to get back to the ball. I didn't even get to dance yet!"

Shelly nodded, and a few sea lavender petals floated away from her hair. She didn't think she could face the queen again, but she knew she had to. She took a deep breath and followed her merfriends.

The Thief Revealed

INSIDE THE PALACE, SHELLY returned to the ballroom, but she didn't approach her aunt. Instead she hid in a corner with Echo and Kiki, sipping shipworm punch. An orchestra of seventeen mermen and merwomen played beautiful music as dancers floated across the floor. François waltzed by with a glass of punch in his hand. He was wearing a sparkling orange mersuit.

"This punch is fin-tastic," Echo said, but to Shelly it tasted like sea mud.

Shelly nearly choked on her drink when Pearl floated up to her with Queen Edwina. "Tell the queen!" Pearl demanded. "Tell her what happened to the Crown of Joy!"

The music screeched to a stop, and everyone turned to stare at Shelly.

Shelly shook her head. "I don't know what happened. The Crown of Joy just disappeared."

Echo whispered Helga's name in Shelly's ear, and Shelly looked up to see the merservant glaring at her. Helga was grumpy and mean, but Shelly couldn't accuse her of taking the tiara when she wasn't sure.

"I know who took it!" Pearl announced.

"Well then, please tell me," Queen Edwina said, "so we can get it back."

Pearl looked around the quiet ballroom and opened her mouth to tell everyone her suspicions.

But to Shelly's surprise, someone else spoke up first.

"I did," Lorelei said.

Sounds of shock came from the crowd. Even Pearl looked stunned.

The queen put her hand over her heart and turned to Lorelei. "But why?"

Lorelei bowed her head. "I was jealous of Shelly."

"Jealous of me?" Shelly asked in wonder.

"I always wanted the Crown of Joy, but Auntie gave it to you instead," Lorelei said softly. "I hid it in my room so you wouldn't be able to wear it. I was going to return it, but then you took my seat at dinner and made Queen Edwina skip our fencing lesson. I was afraid you were taking my place."

Queen Edwina shook her head and held out her arms for Shelly and Lorelei. "Oh, my sweet darlings. No one could ever take either one of your places in my heart. I gave Shelly the crown because it had belonged to her mother."

Relief washed over Shelly as the queen hugged both her nieces. Her aunt wasn't

mad . . . and Shelly hadn't lost the Crown
of Joy after all.

Lorelei patted Shelly's shoulder. "I'm so
sorry. Can you ever forgive me?"

Shelly knew she should have been angry
at her cousin, but she wasn't. Lorelei was

just as scared as she had been. Shelly held her arms out, and Lorelei fell into the hug.

But Queen Edwina had another surprise for Shelly.

"Please forgive me, too," the queen said.

"Whatever for?" Shelly asked.

"For getting so upset. I should have been more understanding," the queen explained. "After all, it's just a crown. And I've lost things myself. How can I make it up to you?"

"There is one thing," Shelly whispered. She was afraid to ask, but this might be her only chance.

"What can I do?" the queen asked.

"Could Lorelei visit me in Trident City?" Shelly asked.

Lorelei's hand flew to her mouth, and

Queen Edwina nodded. "That's an excellent idea, but I'd like to do something for you as well."

Shelly hesitated for just a minute before blurting, "Can you give me fencing lessons too?"

Queen Edwina threw back her head and let out a jolly laugh. "Of course. I insist! Now, we must enjoy the ball." Queen Edwina floated away toward her throne.

"That was so shelltacular!" Pearl said. "You asked the queen for two favors and you got them."

Lorelei hugged Shelly. "Thank you for being so understanding. I know I was mean, but I really am sorry. Cousins and princesses should stick together. I promise that from now on, I'll be the best cousin in the whole merworld."

Shelly smiled. "That sounds totally wave-tastic!" she said with a laugh.

Postcards from Neptune's Castle

★ ✦ ★

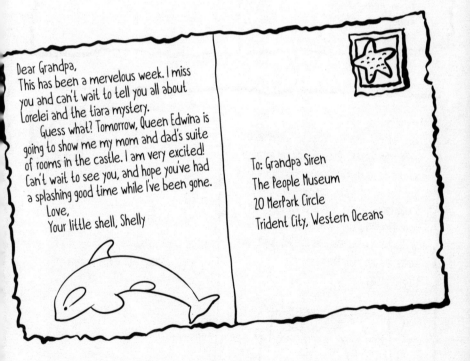

Dear Grandpa,
This has been a mervelous week. I miss
you and can't wait to tell you all about
Lorelei and the tiara mystery.
    Guess what? Tomorrow, Queen Edwina is
going to show me my mom and dad's suite
of rooms in the castle. I am very excited!
Can't wait to see you, and hope you've had
a splashing good time while I've been gone.
    Love,
    Your little shell, Shelly

To: Grandpa Siren
The People Museum
20 MerPark Circle
Trident City, Western Oceans

Dear Crystal,
Guess what? I got to ride a beautiful sea horse. I asked the stable worker, and he told me all the royal sea horses are treated with great care and can leave at any time if they are not happy.

We rode on the sea horses to see a whirlpool. Don't tell Mom and Dad, but it was really, really scary and very exciting. My sea horse was named LilliePoo, and she was bright pink. I hope I will get to visit her again.

Love, your sister,
Echo

Crystal Reef
18 MerPark Circle
Trident City, Western Oceans

Dear Mom,
Guess what? I went to a royal ball with Princess Shelly, Echo, and Kiki. Queen Edwina had her royal tailor make us shelltacular gowns. Mine was gold, just like my tail! I was introduced as Merlady Pearl. It was tails down the best day ever. I even helped solve a mystery! Can't wait to see you to tell you all about it. I know you miss me, but guess what? I miss you and Dad a lot too.

Love, Pearl

Mrs. Swamp
4 MerPark Circle
Trident City, Western Oceans

Dear Mom and Dad,
On my school break, I went with Shelly to visit her great-aunt, Queen Edwina, at Neptune's Castle. We rode sea horses to see an actual whirlpool. I was very scared and shocked at how pretty it was. The water swirled around and around. It was wavy to see, but I hope I never get that close to a whirlpool again.
    Love and miss you, Kiki
    P.S. Please tell my seventeen brothers that I said hi!

Mr. and Mrs. Takeo Coral
557 Ulsan Basin Blvd.
Nereid City, Eastern Oceans

 The Mermaid Tales Song

REFRAIN:

Let the water roar

Deep down we're swimming along

Twirling, swirling, singing the mermaid song.

VERSE 1:

Shelly flips her tail

Racing, diving, chasing a whale

Twirling, swirling, singing the mermaid song.

VERSE 2:

Pearl likes to shine

Oh my Neptune, she looks so fine

Twirling, swirling, singing the mermaid song.

VERSE 3:

Shining Echo flips her tail

Backward and forward without fail

Twirling, swirling, singing the mermaid song.

VERSE 4:

Amazing Kiki

Far from home and floating so free

Twirling, swirling, singing the mermaid song.

Author's Note

WHEN I WAS A YOUNG girl, I loved visiting my grandmother, Lillie Bailey. She had beautiful antique dishes that I thought were so pretty. One day I broke one! I was so afraid that my grandmother would be mad at me. I thought about hiding the dish. Finally I told my grandmother the truth, and she wasn't mad at all!

I thought about my grandmother when

Queen Edwina got upset about the tiara. I believe we should not be wasteful and should take care of our things, but I also believe that people are more important than things. What do you believe?

Your mermaid friend,
Debbie Dadey

Glossary

BEACH MORNING GLORY: This lovely flower grows along the shore.

BELUGA STURGEON: Sturgeon were alive during the time of the dinosaurs, but now they are threatened with extinction.

BLUECHEEK BUTTERFLYFISH: This bright-yellow fish has a blue patch around its eyes. If a coral reef is healthy, it is sure to have many butterflyfish.

BONEFISH: This fish is indeed very bony. It is silvery with dark markings on its back.

BREADCRUMB SPONGE: In deeper waters, this soft sponge has a yellow color.

COLD-WATER CORAL: This is one of just a few reef-forming corals that live in cold water.

CORAL WEED: This red seaweed is dark pink when in the shade and light pink in sunny spots.

DOLPHINFISH: This fast fish can leap out of the water, showing its shiny green back.

EEL: Eels are fish, but they look very much like snakes.

GIANT BRAIN CORAL: This huge coral, which looks like a brain, can live to be hundreds of years old. It can grow to be as wide as a person is tall!

GIANT KELP: Giant kelp is the largest

seaweed in the world. It can grow twenty-four inches in one day!

GULPER EEL: This eel has enormous jaws that allow it to swallow food as big as itself.

HUMP CORAL: This looks like a large, bumpy rock, but it's really a living coral colony that sticks out its tentacles at night to feed.

IRISH MOSS: This is a tough red seaweed that is used to thicken ice cream and yogurt!

KILLER WHALES: Also called orcas, these are sometimes mistaken for whales, but they are actually dolphins. They often hunt in groups and eat fish, squid, seals, and birds.

LADYFISH: This slim, silvery blue fish will skip along the top of the water if alarmed.

PILLOW LAVA: When hot lava oozes out of

ocean crests and meets the cold water, it forms blobs called pillow lava.

RABBITFISH: This fish, also known as a rat fish, is related to sharks. Part of its spine is very poisonous and can inflict serious wounds on humans.

SEA HORSES: Sea horses are small fish that look very much like tiny horses, except with tails instead of legs.

SEA LAVENDER: Common sea lavender grows along the shore.

SEA POTATO: This sea urchin digs in the ground and looks surprisingly like a baked potato.

SHIPWORM: This clam looks more like a worm. It can actually cut into a wooden ship and damage it.

SPECTACULAR SEAWEED: This purple seaweed usually grows in deep water.

TARPON: This fish is related to eels. A single female tarpon can produce twelve million eggs! Tarpon can live for about fifty-five years.

FIND OUT WHAT HAPPENS IN THE NEXT . . .

Mermaid Tales

★Debbie Dadey★

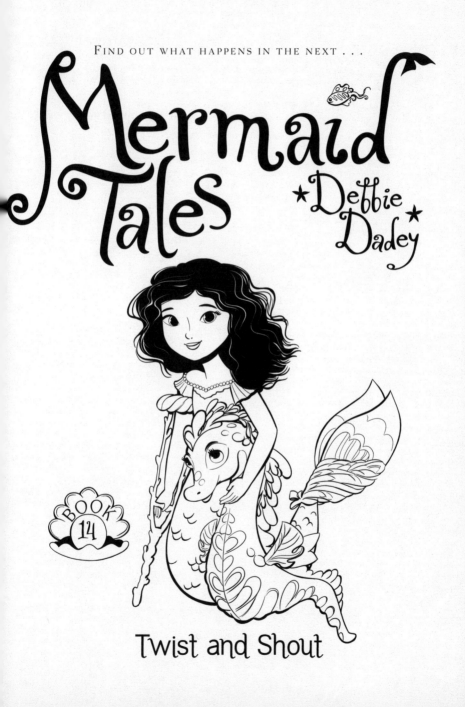

BOOK 14

Twist and Shout

Sea Horses

GREAT JOB ON YOUR KELP reports," Mrs. Karp told her class of third graders. "I'm so glad you enjoyed 'My Side of the Ocean.' It is one of my favorite stories."

Echo tried to pay attention to the lesson, but she couldn't keep her pink tail from tapping the ocean floor. She couldn't wait until school was over! When the final conch shell sounded, Echo soared out of her seat and down the hallway of Trident Academy.

Her best friend, Shelly, followed Echo and patted her shoulder. "Do you have Tail Flippers practice today, or can you come over?"

Echo loved being part of the Tail Flippers dance team, and since the big Poseidon City Dance Competition was coming up next week, Coach Barnacle had been making them practice almost every day after school. Echo's fins ached from all the hard work.

Echo had been working especially hard because she had a big job to do. She was going to perform a very difficult flip called a Scale Dropper. And she was going to do it from the top of a mer-pyramid formed by the other team members! It would be their big finale.

Normally, Echo would have spent her free afternoon at Shelly's home, especially since Shelly lived right above the Trident City People Museum. Echo loved learning about the human world. But there was something else she liked just as much: sea horses!

Echo shook her head. "We don't have practice today, but Rocky invited me to ride one of his sea horses this afternoon."

Shelly smiled. "That sounds fun."

Just then, Coach Barnacle swam by the mergirls. "Well, if it isn't our star Tail Flipper herself! Tell me, Echo, how is your Scale Dropper coming along?"

"Fin-tastic!" Echo told him. "I've even been waking up early to practice it every day before breakfast!"

"Mervelous!" Coach Barnacle boomed. "After all, you're our secret weapon! If you keep practicing, I think our team has a great chance of winning first place."

Coach Barnacle zoomed down the hall just as Rocky burst out of their classroom. He took one look at Echo and grinned. "Shake your tail! It's sea horse time!"

Echo squealed in delight. She waved good-bye to Shelly and sped out of Trident Academy after Rocky. As they swam past the Big Rock Café, Echo's mouth watered at the smell of boxfish burgers. She'd love to have a snack, but she wanted to ride Pinky more.

Pinky was one of Rocky's two sea horses. Zollie was his first sea horse. Rocky's uncle had rescued Zollie from a human's net. Pinky was Zollie's mate, who'd come to stay at Rocky's house too. Echo couldn't help being a tiny bit jealous of Rocky. After all, he had two sea horses and she didn't have any. But at least Rocky was nice enough to let Echo ride Pinky.

The two merkids swam around Rocky's big house and a storage shell to find the two sea horses feeding on small shrimp. When the pets saw Echo and Rocky, they raced over to them. Echo laughed and hugged Pinky while Rocky petted Zollie's head. Soon the merkids were riding on the backs of Pinky and Zollie.

"This is shelltacular!" Rocky yelled. He

leaned down over Zollie's orange neck, urging him to go faster.

Echo did the same to Pinky and yelled, "Giddyup!"

This is what it must be like to be a sailfish, Echo thought. She loved the feeling of water whipping through her curly black hair.

Pinky sprinted through MerPark. Echo waved when she passed Pearl, a girl from her class. Pearl frowned as the two sea horses charged past. "Echo Reef! You'd better slow that thing down!" she snapped.

Echo laughed and shook her head at Pearl. "No wavy way!" she yelled. "This is too much fun!"

But just as Echo turned her head, something horrible happened!

Debbie Dadey

is the author and coauthor of more than one hundred and sixty children's books, including the series The Adventures of the Bailey School Kids. A former teacher and librarian, Debbie and her family live in Sevierville, Tennessee. She hopes you'll visit www.debbiedadey.com for lots of mermaid fun.